THE PAIN IN DADE

BY: ANGEL GREEN

Copyright © 2023 by
Seazons Collections Publishing House.

Copyright © 2023 by Scirocca Publication.

Copyright © 2023 by Angel Green

All rights reserved. No part of this book may be reproduced or used in any manner without written permission of the copyright owner.

Dedication

I would like to thank the Lord up above for bringing me this far in life. To still be here to tell my story to the youth and others!

I would like to dedicate this book to my three wonderful children, Trelaney, Aaliyah and Anthony Jr. Mommy love you guys. This is for you!

To my readers, I would like to thank you for the love and support. As you read through my journey, you will see let nothing get in the way or stop you from loving God and moving on with your life. God will move mountains to place you exactly where you need to be. You can find my book The Pain In Dade on Amazon.com. I hope you guys enjoy.

Contents

Chapter 1	2
Chapter 2	10
Chapter 3	14
Chapter 4	24
Chapter 5	33
Chapter 6	40
Chapter 7	46
Chapter 8	51
Chapter 9	57
Chapter 10	67
Chapter 11	77
The Final Chapter	85

THE PAIN IN DADE

Chapter 1

"James you're not taking my children out of Jacksonville!" Ramona yelled out.

"Romona, this is their family too. The funeral is Saturday. We will be back before you know it." He said.

"If that's the case, I'm going too." Ramona said as she grabbed her suitcase.

"Damn, Mona! Why you have to be so difficult?" He yelled.

"Because I am their mother! And I don't know one that would let her three daughters go hundreds of miles away without going with them." She protested.

"Well, there's a first for everything. I am taking my kids and that's final." Ramona heard the firmness in James voice. "Listen, Mona. I know you're worried. But they will be fine. We'll be back before you know it. Just trust me. Ok?" He said in a more settled tone. Hesitatingly she agreed.

The next morning, James packed the girls up and left. The drive was well over eight hours. James checked into a hotel, freshened the kids up and headed to the service. "Alright, y'all listen up. We going to walk in this church and pay our respect. You get to see a few of your kin folk while we here. Now come on." He said.

The funeral lasted every bit of two hours. The girls was tired and they wanted their mom. "Dad, are we going home now?" Rochelle asked. Rochelle was James and Ramona's eldest child. She was every spit of Ramona.

"Just set back there with your sisters. Y'all take a nap." James turned the radio on, crunk up the car and drove off.

The Pain in Dade

When the girls woke up, they heard their father arguing with some woman. "James, you should be ashamed of yourself bringing them children all the way to Miami. I already have Jewel occasionally, what the hell I suppose to do with three more! I am done raising kids." The older woman spat.

Rochelle leaned forward and looked out the window. "Rochelle, where are we?" Raeven asked.

"I don't know but I'm about to find out." She whispered. "Stay here with Rhiley. I'll be back." She said. Just as she was opening the door, James walked up and snatched it open.

"Y'all come on. Rochelle, get your sisters and take them in the house while I get these bags." Sweat was profusely pouring down his face.

"Dad, where are we?" Raeven asked.

"At your grandma house." He stated.

"But I thought we was going home." Rochelle said with tear filled eyes.

"Look here, don't question me. Take your behinds in

Angel Green

the house and sat on the couch. I'll be in there in a second!" He said in agitated tone. The girls did as they were told. They knew if they didn't, an ass whooping was coming next. They walked in the house and sat on the plastic wrapped couch.

"Mama?" James called out.

"Yea, boy! What you want?" She called from the kitchen.

"I'm putting the girls stuff in my room. They sitting out here on the settee. I'm about to run down to Otis and have a drink. I'll be back."

"And what the hell they suppose to eat?" She yelled out.

"Ain't you cooking?" He sighed.

"Yeah. Enough for me and the one you got back yonder in that back room." James rolled his eyes.

"Listen, don't pay that no mind. Your grandma going to feed you. I need to run out for a minute. Y'all eat and Rochelle make sure they get their bath. Then y'all go to sleep. Daddy will see y'all later." He palmed their tiny faces and planted kisses on their foreheads. Then just like that, he left.

Moments later, Cora made her way into the living room. "I know damn well, y'all no good daddy left y'all. After I told him not to." She said placing her hands on her hips. Rochelle, Rhiley and Raeven just stared at her. "Jewel, come out here!" Cora called out.

"Yes, grandma?" She said quickly walking down the hallway.

"I want you to meet your sisters. Y'all introduce yourselves to Jewel. She's your daddy's oldest child." Rochelle looked at Raeven and frowned. She thought she was their father's first born.

"I'm Rochelle." She said in a low tone.

"I'm Rhiley." She smiled slyly.

"Nice to meet you." Jewel smiled.

"And you are?" Cora squinted her eyes. Raeven didn't bulge. Rochelle nudged her in the side.

"Raeven." She answered.

Angel Green

"Raeven, huh?" Cora eyed her sideways. "Well Ms. Raeven, from the looks of it, it sound like you're the one I'm going to have a problem out of. But I want you to hear me loud and clear. I don't mind getting a switch off one of those trees and putting something on your little behind. This is my house and I'm doing y'all daddy a father. So, don't forget it." She wagged her finger. "Now Jewel, take them to their room. Then get them in that kitchen so they can eat some supper."

"Yes, ma'am." Jewel did as she was told.

When they got in the room, Jewel eased the door shut. "If y'all don't want to get any spanking, I suggest you do exactly what she tell y'all to do. And don't give her no lip. Just do it." She whispered.

"I want my mom." Raeven shouted.

"Shhh! Now you must be want a spanking." Raeven shook her head no. "Then stop all of that. Now I am telling you, I've been staying here for years and the only way to survive in this hell hole is to do exactly what you are told. Now do y'all got that?" Everyone agreed except Raeven. Jewel knew exactly how she felt. So, she couldn't blame her. There were many nights that she cried for her mom. But letting Cora see her cry was not the best thing to do.

"So, where are we? And why is it so hot?" Rochelle asked.

"That's the best part of Miami. The heat ain't no joke." Jewel laughed.

"Y'all get y'all behinds in here! This supper getting cold!" Cora yelled out. "And after you finish eating, I want that little fast one with the pink bows in her head to help clean this kitchen."

"Better get use to it." Jewel whispered.

The girls all did their chores and got ready for bed. "So Jewel, do you live here or are you just visiting?" Rochelle asked.

"I live with my mom. She doesn't live too far from here. But every so often, I come stay with grandma when daddy's home from the Navy." Jewel explained.

"I see." Rochelle sighed.

"Well we better get to bed before daddy get home. Goodnight." Jewel smiled gracefully. Rochelle closed her eyes and said a prayer. Then she finally dozed off.

The next morning, James was packing his bags when the girls walked into the living room. "We leaving daddy? We going back to mommy?" Raeven asked in excitement.

"No. I have to get back on Navy base. You three are going to stay here with your grandmama." He said firmly. The girls looked at each other. They were confused to why they were even their. They knew nothing about this place. They wanted to go home. But protesting was the last thing they knew they should do. They watched as James hugged Cora. He placed a wad of bills in her hand. She smiled gracefully.

"Now you just gone ahead. These girls will be just fine." She said. James placed a kids on all of his little ladies and was out the door.

Chapter 2

Months had passed since the girls last saw James. He would call every chance he'd got. The girls missed him so much. Living with Cora was like living in hell. She began treating Raeven as if she wasn't her grandchild. "Raeven, if I tell you again, I'm going to drag you by that long hair." Cora threatened.

"Grandma, I've cleaned that spot."

"Are you being sassy Raeven?" She asked wagging her finger.

"No ma'am." Raeven dropped her head. Raeven felt as though her grandmother didn't like her much. She wanted to express herself to Rochelle and Rhiley, but it wasn't easy talking to them. They're bond were close. The only person who seemed to have treated Raeven like someone was Jewel.

"The ugly duckling in there cleaning up again." Rochelle laughed.

"She must've gotten in trouble in school today." Rhiley laughed.

As time went on Raeven found herself getting spankings for things Rochelle and Rhiley would do. Raeven felt as though she wasn't even their sister. She didn't feel like it was right, but Cora seemed to like every bit of it. As Raeven sat in the mirror brushing her hair, she thought about what Cora had mentioned to her regarding a time when she was in Head Start. Cora told her she didn't like it. Raeven remember getting a spanking everyday for acting out in school. But the only reason she acted out was because of the treatment she got at home. But that wasn't the only discipline she got. Raeven's hair flowed down her back freely. That was a beauty trait she inherited from her mother. It was full and lengthy. However, Cora accused her of lying so much and as punishment she would cut Raeven's hair each time she felt she was lying.

"Cora, that Raeven is such a beautiful little thing. I want to be her God mother. With all that pretty long hair, she's going to break many hearts when she get older." Irene said. Irene was Cora's best friend.

"You talking about this little lying thing right here?" Cora asked pointing her finger at Raeven. "If she still lying so much and listen to them teachers, she'll be alright. As a matter of fact, get your butt up and go in the room." Cora looked at Raeven wickedly. Raeven did as she was told.

"Now Cora, she can't be that bad. I got a few of my own and from the looks of it, she ain't no where near how they knucklehead asses are." They both laughed.

"Well Mother Goose, if you want to be her God mother, you go right ahead." Cora said. They both laughed at Cora's sarcasm.

The next day, Irene came by and brought Raeven some clothes and toys. "What do you say?" Cora asked

Raeven.

"Thank you." Raeven smiled.

"You're welcome baby. But God mama have to run. I got some business to handle. I'll see you later pretty girl."

When Irene left, Cora found fault in something Raeven had done. "See that's why you don't earn anything. You don't listen! Give those clothes and toys to Rochelle and Rhiley. Then take your little behind back there in that room!" She said. Raeven's heart broke. She cried silently as she laid in bed. She knew if Cora heard her crying, she would get a beating. It was unfair. No birthday's, no Christmas gifts, no love. If Irene and Jewel didn't buy it, Cora wasn't at all. Raeven just couldn't understand why. Jewel was like her guardian Angel. She was always there and Raeven loved her for that.

Chapter 3

After a few years, James had finally come home from the Navy for good. Raeven was happy because she knew he would protect her and have her back. But, things went a different way. One night James had come home from the bar. He was drunk and saying all kind of things. Just like Grandpa. "James, you got to do something with that Raeven. That girl is little liar and I don't like it." Cora said.

"What she do, mama?" He asked.

"What don't she do! She ain't like the others. Just want to do what she wants to do. That teacher say she so bad. You need to put her behind in her place."

Angel Green

"Bring her here." He slurred.

When Raeven walked in the room, she didn't know what to expect. James was sitting on the edge of the bed. She knew Cora had made things up that she didn't even do. "What's this I hear yours being bad in school and around the house." He questioned.

"I don't be bad, daddy. It's just…"

"It's just what, Raeven! You think you grown?" Raeven could smell the liquor coming out his pores.

"No." She shook her head disagreeably.

"Climb up in that bed." Raeven could barely understand what he was saying. James eased in bed behind Raeven. She felt his hand crawl up her nightgown and into her panties. She jumped and began shaking. "When you be bad in school and around the house, I will teach you." He stuck his fingers inside her tiny opening. Tears began to escape her eyes. "It feel good?" He painted. Raeven didn't say a word. James popped her. "I asked you a question?" She shook her head yes. All she knew is whatever he was doing, she wanted it to be over. She couldn't understand why he was doing this. "If you ever tell anybody, I will kill you." He rolled over and fell asleep. Raeven cried silently. She was afraid. She just wanted to die at that moment. She wanted to kill herself. She closed her eyes tight and fell asleep.

The next day, Raeven went to school as though nothing happened. "Why you're so quiet and sitting over here by yourself? Are you ok?" Misty asked. Misty and Raeven was best friends. They told each other everything. But this was one thing Raeven couldn't tell. She was afraid that James would kill her.

"I'm ok." She lied.

"Doesn't seem that way." Misty shrugged.

"I am. Just tired." Raeven sighed. Truth was, she wasn't ok. But she was happy to be at school and out of that house. School was her getaway from James and Cora. Rochelle and Rhiley also went to the same school.

Raeven loved school. Her favorite subject was P.E. and math; Mr. Mike's class. She had the best teachers ever until one day, Ms. Zoey decided to call James. When he walked into the class, Raeven's heart skipped a beat. "You think you grown in this lady class cursing! Stand up!" He yelled. Raeven didn't even think Ms. Zoey heard her. When she stood up, James beat her in front of everyone. "Laugh at her!" He told the class. Even those who wasn't laughing, starting laughing. "Let me speak to her outside and I'll send her back in." He told Ms. Zoey. When the door closed he looked at Raeven. "And you know that ain't all." He wagged his finger. "Now get back in there." Ms. Zoey didn't know what she had done. It was going to be hell to pay when she got home. Raeven looked at the clock and a lump formed in her throat. She didn't want to go home. She wanted to run away. But she didn't know how or where to go. So instead, she faced the consequences.

A few days later, Misty and Raeven was at the playground talking about Mr. Summer's upcoming test when Bella walked up. "What y'all over here talking about?" She asked.

"That stupid test." Misty rolled her eyes. "I got to use the restroom. Raeven you going with me?"

"No. I'm good." Raeven answered.

The Pain in Dade

"Ok. I'll be back."

"Why you look so sad? Like you want to run away." Bella laughed.

"I do." Raeven mumbled. Instantly, Bella knew she was serious because she didn't crack a smile. The look Raeven had was all familiar to her.

"I know that look you're wearing. I wear it often. So if you plan on running away, just make sure you serious. I use run away all the time and not get caught." Bella shook her head.

"Where do you go?" Raeven was all ears.

"It depends where I end up."

The girls talked a little longer and came up with a plan. Just as they had finished talking Misty walked up. "You ready?" She asked.

"Yea. See you later Bella." Raeven winked. Bella nodded her head and smiled.

Raeven and Misty walked to Raeven's house. Raeven didn't tell her the plan she had, but she did tell her she wanted to go to her house for a little bit but she had to ask her dad. When they arrived at Raeven's house, James was in the living room watching TV and Cora was in the kitchen.

"Dad, we have a project that we have to do together and I wanted to know if I can go to Misty house to work on it?" She asked.

"Why y'all can't stay here and do it?" He questioned.

"Because her mom said she can't. She have to do it at home." James didn't say anything. He kept looking at the TV. Raeven walked in the kitchen where Cora was and explained.

"You just make sure you back before them street lights come on. You hear me?"

"Yes, ma'am." Raeven nodded.

As the girls started walking down the road they both looked at each and said, "I have something to tell you". They laughed.

"You first." Raeven said.

"One day I came to your house with my mom to see if you was home. My mom stayed in the car. I knocked on the door and your dad told me to come in. He started getting real fresh with me. I was scared. I told him I just wanted to know if you was home and I had to go! That's why I don't like coming to your house." She started crying. By that time, the girls had made it to the park. They both were on the bench crying, hugging each other. "What did you have to tell me?" She asked. Raeven was scared to say because she knew if she mumbled a word, James would kill her. "It's ok. Tell me." Misty said when she saw the fear in Raeven's eyes. Raeven took a deep breath and told her everything. "I knew something was wrong how you be so sad in school. We have to tell someone."

"No!!" Raeven yelled.

"Why not!" Misty shouted.

"He will kill me! Please don't! I am going to handle it! That's why I wanted to come to your house! Please!" Raeven begged.

"What are you going to do?" Misty asked with tear filled eyes.

"I'm going to run away!"

Angel Green

"And where are you going to go?" She asked.

"Bella house." Tears fell freely from both of their eyes.

"You think you have this all planned out?"

"Yes!" Raeven nodded. "But please tell me you're not going to say anything to anyone. Not even your mom." They both pinky sweared.

HONK! HONK!

It was time for Misty to go home. Her mom had come. She asked Raeven if she needed a ride. She told her no, she was ok. She would walk. Misty walked Raeven to the corner. The girls hugged. "Be careful." Misty said. In her area, people got raped and killed.

"I will."

"I love you." Misty said trying to hold back her tears.

"I love you too." The girls hugged one last time and went on their way.

Misty lived down the street from Bella. Which was convenient. When Raeven got to Bella's house, they stayed in until it got dark. Her parents didn't mind because her mom was on crack and her dad drunk a lot. "Walk with me to do the park." Bella said.

"Ok." Raeven was with it. They was free to do and go where they wanted. But what she went to the park for, Raeven wasn't with it. So, she went back home and took the whooping. Raeven was happy James was out of town. He couldn't hurt her.

"Why did your little grown ass do that!" Cora yelled. Raeven knew this was her moment of truth.

"Because I'm tired of being touched on by daddy. He locks me up in that room and feel on me."

POP!

Cora slapped her. "You're a liar! You want attention! That's what you want! Get your ass out my face and go in that room!" Raeven was hurt. She was telling the truth and Cora didn't believe her. It felt as though she was working with him. Raeven feared she was going to tell James when he got home. But she didn't. However, things got even worse. He was no longer sticking his fingers inside of her. This time it was his penis.

"Argh!!!!" Raeven screamed loud. She was sure Rochelle, Rhiley, and Cora heard her. But no one came to her rescue. James had took her world. She was bleeding bad and he didn't care. Raeven was only seven years old. But it kept going on when she was eleven too. Thankfully, she didn't get pregnant from him. Raeven couldn't understand, how the one you love can do this to you.

Chapter 4

The following day when it was time for school, it was girls and boys day. Where the boys go play games and the girls sit in a circle and talk with the teacher. Ms. Williams asked us what was the consequences at home when we are bad in school. She enjoyed the stories about how we got spankings. She was mean but she was fun and an understanding teacher. We all sat and listened to each other's stories as we ate popcorn. When it was Raeven's turn, she had nothing to say. She dropped her head. Misty nudged her in the side and gave her that look. "It's time." She whispered. Misty knew this was Raeven's chance to tell the right person. "Ms. Williams, can me and Raeven speak with you outside?"

"Sure." She got up and walked the girls out. Instantly, Raeven broke down in tears and told everything. Ms. Williams heart went out to Raeven. She held on to Raeven for dear life as if she was her parent. She could feel her pain. Ms. Williams fought back her tears. "Raeven, I'm going to walk you down to the nurse. Misty, go back inside with the girls. We'll be back."

Raeven was in so much pain. When they got to the clinic area, Ms. Williams walked her inside, talked to the lady and left. The lady looked at Raeven. "Are you ok?"

"No." She whispered.

"Raeven, you will be ok. I'm not a nurse. I work undercover for H.R.S. for kids like you that's being abused." Raeven's heart skipped a beat. She knew this wasn't good. She immediately told the lady what James had told her. She didn't want this to get out. But the lady assured her, everything was going to be ok. Raeven was scared.

The bell had ring. It was time for her to go home. On

the way home, Rochelle noticed something was wrong. "Why you walking so slow?" She asked. But Raeven couldn't say anything. When they turned the corner on their street, it looked like every news station was there and the lady from the school. The moment Raeven walked in the yard, James grabbed her arm. "You remember what I said I'm going to do right?" He said it loud enough so that only he and Raeven could hear. "Cora is going to be mad as hell when she get home." He said.

The lady from the school called Cora and told her she needed to get home. And she came fast. "Y'all believe this little lying thing if you want to!" Cora was loud talking. "All she do is lie! Tell them people you lying!" She yelled.

"Well ma'am, we will be able to tell at the rape center." The lady assured her. And that's exactly where they went. Rochelle and Rhiley had to be tested too. Raeven's and Rochelle's insides were messed up. Rhiley was never touched. They placed James in jail. Ms. Williams was fighting to have custody of the girls. She didn't want them split up or taken by H.R.S., but it didn't work. They placed the girls in a foster home in Carol City. Far away from Cora. The girls knew nothing about the town because they was from down south. The lady who ran the house name was Ms. Cohen. She was not nice and the girls wasn't nice to her either. There was other kids in the house. Three boys and one girl. The front of the house was cool. But the back part of the house where the girls were told to sleep was dusty and not cleaned. Ms. Cohen had built extra rooms back there and that's where the girls had to sleep. It was bunk beds and little class room chairs where they were told to eat at as if they were animals. The girls didn't like it one bit. They slept in one bed and cried themselves to sleep.

The next day she took them to register for school. She registered Raeven first being that she was in elementary. Then she registered the other two in high school. The girls didn't get along with others because they wasn't from this area. And they weren't good with making new friends.

One day, Rochelle had beef with some girls. They followed Rochelle and Rhiley to Raeven's school. One of the girls ran up and hit Rochelle. Rochelle turned around started swinging. A few others was holding Rhiley, while the others began jumping Rochelle. "Oooh Raeven! They out there jumping your sister." Freddy yelled as he looked out the window. Raeven was in her last class of the day; reading. When she looked out the window, her eyes grew the size of quarters.

"Ms. Guston, may I leave?" She asked.

"No. You leave when the bell ring." Raeven looked at her and walked out the door. One thing her father and grandma always taught them, was stick together. She ran full speed down the road, but by the time she got there, it was over. Raeven was yelling and cursing. One of the boys ran up and told her to calm down. Even though they had jumped Rochelle, she got them. They couldn't handle her. They had to cut her in order to slow her down. The girls went into the office and called the police. They couldn't make the report without their foster mother being present. So the police drove to the house and the girls walked.

"They only fault you because the girl Samantha that

lives with y'all told them girls that the boy like Rochelle." The boy Johnny said as he walked with them. The girls looked at each other. They knew exactly what they had to do. When they got home, they all talked to the police. He took the report and left. The girls tried to tell Ms. Cohen it was Samantha's fault. But she paid them no mind. So, they took matters into their own hands.

"Why did you get those girls to jump my sister!" Raeven boldly asked.

"Because I did!" Samantha said in a slick tone. Raeven punched her with a quickness. Then Rochelle and Rhiley followed. Ms. Cohen heard the commotion and tried her best to break up the fight but failed to do so. She called the H.R.S. caseworker and she came out. She was able to get the situation under control. She was the only one the girls listened to.

"They can't stay here! I'm scared if you leave them here, it will get worse" Ms. Cohen yelled. The caseworker, packed the girls up. She took Rochelle and Rhiley to a program for girls and boys and placed Reaeven in another home. They were split up. Raeven didn't like that. So, she'll run away in attempt to find Rochelle and Rhiley. Of course the police caught her and they placed her in another home. One lady had room and she allowed Raeven to come there. She was cool but Raeven had to see her sisters. She missed them. She overheard the caseworker and the lady talking. The caseworker told her that Rochelle and Rhiley was at Brige. Raeven knew where it was. So she was on a mission to find them.

Raeven ran away. But she felt sick. The lady was worried. She didn't know where Raeven was. She called the police and the caseworker. They finally caught her and took her to the hospital. "Why did you run away?" The caseworker asked.

"I want to see Rochelle and Rhiley." Raeven admitted.

"I was going to take you the very next day." When they left the hospital, the caseworker took her to see them. Raeven was happy. But that was her last time she saw them.

After a while, they placed Raeven in another home. She kept running away until she ran away with these group of girls. They wen to the Flea Market to meet some boys. One of the boys liked Raeven. But Raeven was trying to get out of that city. It was a bad area and she was from down south. "Hey Kesha, I'm about to go." Raeven said.

"Why? We having fun girl." She said.

"Yeah but I'm not feeling it. I'll catch y'all later." Just as Raeven was about to leave, one of the guys pulled out a gun.

"You ain't going no damn where." He said pointing the gun. The other girls looked scared. Raeven looked at him. "Get on your knees and suck this dick." He ordered. Raeven was twelve and he was about fifteen. She was scared. She got down her knees and into position. The boy that liked Raeven intervened.

"Man, stop that shit!" He yelled. When the boy turned, Raeven noticed the gun didn't have a clip in it. She jumped to her feet and took off running. He ran behind her. The boy that like Raeven pushed him. "Run!" He yelled. And Raeven did just that. Raeven saw a bus coming in the distance. When it came to a stop, she got on it. There, she was safe. Raeven knew if he would've had a clip, he was going to kill her. But

The Pain in Dade

God had other plans for her.

Chapter 5

Eventually, Raeven got tired of running away and turned herself in. She was placed in a home for a while. One day, the caseworker called and said she had a placement for Raeven and Rhiley was coming. Finally, they were going to be together. Raeven was ecstatic. She took them to this lady name Ms. Lorna's house. The lady seemed so nice but the minute the caseworker left, she changed. But it didn't bother the girls. They had been through so much. All they wanted was each other.

One day while getting ready for church, Ms. Lorna had a baby in the home. Then Raeven and Rhiley was watching the baby while Lorna was getting dressed.

"Ms. Lorna, we're hungry!" Rhiley said.

"I said, wait!" She yelled. Rhiley sat on the baby. They all laughed. The baby started crying. Lorna came in the room. They didn't care. They was hungry. "Take y'all behind outside!" She yelled. The girls were happy because they hadn't been outside since they been there. Looking around, they realized they were across the street from South Ridge High School. That's where Rochelle attended. So they came up with a plan to run away.

"On the count of three, we're going to run across to that field." When Raeven did the countdown, Raeven took off running. Rhiley just stood there. When she heard Ms. Lorna coming out of the house, she took off running. They ran all the way to Rochelle's house. She was standing on the porch. When she saw them, her face lit up with joy.

"Our foster mom is probably looking for us. She stay around the corner. We got to get away from here." Rhiley said.

"Come on." Rochelle took them over to their grandma's house. She wasn't home but their grandpa was there. He was so drunk, he never knew they even left.

When Rhiley looked out the window, she saw the police coming up the street. "Damn." She whispered. "We got to hide y'all." The girls jumped up and looked for hiding places. Rhiley hid in the attic, Rochelle hid in the closet and Raeven hid under the baby crib. The police knocked on the door. Grandpa opened the door.

"Hello, Sir. We are looking for three young ladies. Your granddaughters to be exact. Are they here?"

"No!" He lied.

"If they are, you going to jail." The officer assured.

"Fuck y'all. They not here."

"Can we look around?" One of the officers asked.

"Go right ahead. I told you they not here." The police looked around. The first person they spotted was Rhiley

The Pain in Dade

"We know you are in here. So you might as well come out." They couldn't find them in their safe places but they just surrendered. "Why did y'all run away?"

"Lorna doesn't feed us and we wanted to see our grandma." Rhiley explained.

They took them all back to placement so that they could be placed in another home. They stayed there for three days because no one wanted to take all three of them. They placed Rhiley and Rochelle together. Raeven was placed alone again. Raeven didn't understand why she was left alone. She was the baby. But every chance she got, she ran away. And so did Rhiley and Rochelle. Eventually they got tired of looking for them and only came when they got in trouble.

After a few months, they placed Rhiley and Rochelle back with Cora. But Raeven was still in the system. She continued to run away but was then placed in Ms. Jacob's residence. Raeven actually liked it there. That's where she learned to pimp girl's; at the age of 13. It was a four bedroom home. The cleanest house Raeven was ever placed in. There was three rooms in the front.

Angel Green

One belong to Ms. Jacob and her mother. That's where they slept. In the other two rooms there were about six girls. The room in the back is the room Raeven shared with another girl and her baby. They even had their own bathroom. It was nice at first. Raeven didn't want to listen to anyone or go to school because she didn't like that school. So, Ms. Jacobs called the caseworker. The caseworker talked things out with Raeven and she made up her mind to go to school. She end up liking the school because she loved basketball. She joined the team. Raeven was the best at anything she did.

She started getting alone with some of the girls at the house. One, she had to put in their place. Raeven didn't like how she was popping off at the mouth, so she had to get her together. Raeven had a mix of her mother and father in her. She was half white and half black. The girl called her white, but she cut it short when Raeven beat her ass. Raeven knew black folks didn't like white folks back in the days. So her and her siblings didn't like to be called white. They couldn't help the fact that their mother was white. But they was black and that was that!

The Pain in Dade

After a while, Raeven started letting the girls firm the house go with her on the weekends. Raeven was cool with the guys because thats who took care of her. They called her Baby G because she was a little gangsta. Raeven started selling the girls to the guys. She would boost their confidence up just so they could feel good about themselves. Raeven would make good money. With her cut, she started buying weed and beer. Ms. Jacobs loved Raeven as if she was really her own. Raeven kept the house clean and even helped bought food. H.R.S. would be late sometimes giving Ms. Jacob the checks, so Raeven was a big help to her.

"Raeven how do you get that much money?" She asked.

"I pimp the girls." Raeven admitted. Ms. Jacobs laughed.

"Well if they let you do that, that is on them." She said.

Raeven cooked, kept the house clean and everyone went to school. That was the best foster home she had ever been in. It felt like the family she was missing. That's why she never ran away. Staying in Ms. Jacobs's home, Raeven learned a lot and she met different people. Ms. Jacobs daughter loved Raeven and she treated her as if she was her own. She called Raeven her God daughter. That made Raeven feel good even though she wasn't her real mother. She prayed that she would adopt her but it never happened. Raeven never knew her real mother but she was ok with her newly found God mother.

Chapter 6

As time moved on, Raeven felt it was time to move on. She ended up running away and staying in a home that was near her grandma's house. Raeven attended Jr. Lee Middle School. There, she knew a few people out there. There was a click out there they called Sugar Hill Posy (S.H.P.). They also had a nasty version of it, Sweet Harry Pussy. The age range was from ten to fifteen years old. When Raeven hooked up with them, they taught her things they knew and things she didn't know. They were from the same town, just different parts. They stayed across the tracks and Raeven stayed across Alppatler. But it's the same town called Glouds. Which was Miami; the city.

Angel Green

Everyday they would skip school during lunchtime and go to the corner store to get chips and candy. There was these guys outside the store that use to talk to them. Raeven would never talk to them because they were too old and she wasn't into older guys. But there was this one guy in particular that would be at the store. Raeven knew him from math class. She kind of likes him. His name was Terrell. He was handsome and smart. She later discovered he sold drugs but that didn't make a difference because she was doing the same thing.

When they left talking to the boys, Raeven and the girls would jump on the train and go to the mall to steal out of Macy's. It was a breeze until one day they got caught. It seemed like all the females from school was in the stealing. Some of them went in the dressing room putting clothes underneath their clothes or stuffing them down in their clothes. Then they would try to walk out the door. Some of them slipped up and went out two different doors and still got caught. Raeven wasn't going out that easy. She took off running because jail wasn't an option. She wouldn't have gotten caught if the security guard didn't jump in the car and chased her down. They took everybody back to the school on the patty wagon. They got ten days out of school and five days indoor suspension. But they didn't care. They didn't want to be in school anyway.

Raeven's boyfriend Terrell wasn't too fond of her getting in trouble. He was mad when they all got back to school. "You need to stay out of trouble." He said.

"I will." She laughed. But he didn't crack a smile.

"I'm serious." He looked at her.

"Ok." Raeven started listening to him because she loved him and she knew he loved her too.

One day, she was waiting for him to show up for school but he never came. She didn't hear from him at all. That wasn't like Terrell. Then, his mother had informed her that he was killed in a drive by shooting. Her heart dropped. She had lost her best friend. Someone who actually cared for her. She lost it.

Everyday she would get into fights, stealing, selling drugs, and stealing cars. She even dropped out of school in the ninth grade and started doing her own

Angel Green

thing. She completely lost it. She stayed in the street. She didn't go back to the foster home. She would stay wherever she was able to lay her head. The niggas on the street called her Baby G. The only thing that was on her mind was getting money.

A guy name Lion from Richmond Heights offered Raeven a proposition. "You want a side job?" He asked.

"What I have to do?" She asked.

"Just watch out for me and Bray while we hit a Nigga across the head. When you see the police you holla yeeooooo! And we will get missing." He explained.

"Ok. I'm with it. How much you paying?"

"Don't worry, you'll like the pay. You just meet us at the park after the jobs are done."

Everything went exactly how Lion said. Raeven would watch out and they would meet at the park, get fucked up, talk junk to each other and then the rest of their click would come out there and they would all play basketball and chill. Then repeat it all the next day. Raeven was the only female in the group. She was a little thug getting money.

One day, while chilling at the park a girl that Raeven use to refer to as her sister came up to her. "Did you hook Rhiley up with Anthony?" She asked with attitude.

"Girl get the fuck out of my face!" Raeven spat. The girl swung at Raeven but missed. That was the wrong move because Raeven beat the hell out of her. Then her sister jumped in. That was the only way they knew they could get Raeven. When Lion got word, he called up Rhiley. A guy named Wesley took them to the girl's house. Raeven them was put numbered. It was eight of them and four on Raeven's side. But that didn't mean anything because Raeven and her sisters beat their ass. Rhiley had a bat and their mother tried to jump in. But Rochelle beat the lady with the bat. It was crazy. They called the police and Raeven and the rest jumped in the car and went to their dad's house to hide out. When everything calmed down, they went back to the park to see if them bitches was going to be there. But they wasn't. Raeven got dope off the park with the boys and then Rhiley them left.

Angel Green

The weekend was over and she had to g wet back on her grind. Raeven sold drugs until they sent her off to Job Corps. They thought it was going to change her but only made her worse….

Chapter 7

Raeven was sixteen years old when she went up to Job Corps. Rhiley was already up there. They was both happy to see each other. When Raeven got there, she became home sick the minute she got off the van.

"I'm so happy you here!" Rhiley beamed with joy the moment they saw each other.

"Me too sis." Raeven smiled. Rhiley introduced her to a few of her friends and then helped her put her things up in the dorm. Then, she took Raeven to meet the boy she was planning on marrying. After, Rhiley took her to Coach Jay. He was the basketball coach. He told Raeven to come to the next meeting so he can her skills. Immediately after he saw her play, she was apart of the team.

Raeven took up Culinary Arts and GED classes. At first she was all in until she became lazy. Raeven wasn't listening to anyone. Not even Rhiley. She became buck wild. They end up calling Raeven's step mom to get permission to administer her some medication. Raeven wasn't crazy. She just was a little hyper. That medicine didn't work. She was still the same person. They tried to help but, it didn't work.

One day, Raeven found out through a girl at the center, that this girl named Naomi liked Rhiley. Raeven told her what she had heard. Then someone ran and told Roger; her boyfriend. He got mad wanted to fight Naomi. Job Corp center was zero tolerance when it came to fighting. When the dorm manager found out, they had a meeting with all three of them. Since Rhiley was finished with her trade and had already gotten her GED, they made her go home. Raeven didn't think that was fair. But it was ok because Rochelle was talking about coming up. Raeven went back to the dorm with Rhiley and helped her packed.

The Pain in Dade

Rhiley called Rochelle and gave her the bad news. She was mad but it was cool because Raeven was still there.

As Raeven was walking down the hallway, she spotted Naomi. "That's why, my other sister Rochelle, going to take your nigga!" Raeven yelled. And that's exactly what Rochelle did. Together, Rochelle and Raeven was a crazy duo. They didn't listen to no one and they as bad as hell. Rhiley was the good one.

One day, Rochelle and Raeven was smoking weed, walking around the pool and Rhiley wanted to hit the weed. After she took a puff, she lost her mind. Her crazy butt started running around the pool.

"Jody don't let her ass hit the weed no more. She going to get us caught. Calm your ass down girl." Raeven yelled. After that, Rhiley was cool. They were bad as ever. When they went to class, they'll climb under the desk and write their names. Either saying, Rochelle was here or Raeven was here. And other sayings like, Dade County. Just so everyone knew where they was from. Then they would go to sleep.

Then one day, Raeven fell asleep. Rochelle left her in class and went to GED class. Rochelle was focused on her work. So Raeven didn't have a sleeping buddy anymore. So, Raeven started bucking down, doing her work. Raeven had straighten up when Rochelle came. When Rhiley was there, she wasn't hanging with Raeven like that because again, she was the good one. She wasn't with getting into trouble. She was getting good grades. Raeven thought she was an ass kisser. But eventually she understood why. Getting those good grades caused them to get money from the center. If you was new, you'll get three flying tens and red was considered twenty dollars. Whereas, green was thirty dollars. Silver and gold was one hundred dollars. Rhiley was always gold. Rochelle and Raeven stayed in red. Raeven managed to get green one time.

When Rochelle came, a few more girls came behind her. One of the girls name was June. She looked just like a boy. Raeven use to mess with her everyday. One day, she was in the shower and Raeven went to take a shower. When Raeven saw June in the shower, she screamed. "Mrs. Avery, there's a boy in the dorm!" Raeven yelled. Mrs. Avery came searching, only to find June. Raeven got in trouble. But she didn't care.

The Pain in Dade

One day while Raeven was playing basketball on the gym, June walked in and asked to play. Surprisingly, she was good. And from there, her and Raeven hit it off. They became best friends. Rochelle was happy that Raeven had made a friend because Raeven use to mess with June every day. Hurting her feelings. But when they became best friends, they realized, they were just alike. They both knew how to ball. They would talk about people and dared them say anything. They had become a team.

They end up getting a dog that wasn't too fond of black people. His name was Boomar. There was a store inside center where you could buy snacks and food. One day, Raeven and June walked to the store and saw Boomar. They managed to get Boomar to go behind the building with them. They beat him real bad. After that, he loved black people and Pops never knew why.

Chapter 8

They had turned Job Corps out. Rochelle had gotten into a fight with Naomi. The same girl whose boyfriend she had stole. Rochelle was in trade when someone came and told her Naomi was out there trying to talk to him. That was something they didn't play in Miami. So Naomi had to get beat. They never got caught for fighting and they dared anyone to tell.

Raeven's days at Lyndon B. Johnson Job Corp was numbered. She was kicked out for drinking on her birthday. But she didn't care because she was ready to go home anyways. They still gave Raeven her money for completing the trade but she didn't get her GED.

The Pain in Dade

Raeven was young. Her only focus was on getting money. So she went back home and moved back with her dad and his wife. His wife tried to make her go to school but Raeven wasn't listening to her. She felt she wasn't her mother, so why listen.

When she got ready, Raeven enrolled herself up to school. Back in the days, you didn't need a parent to sign you up. School was an escape for Raeven to get away from her father's wife. She started focusing on her work because a part of her really wanted to finish. However, she kept getting in trouble by smoking weed and skipping school. Some days she would leave school and go on the block and set up shop. Just to make money to eat and give James money for living with him. That was Raeven's everyday routine until she hooked back up with Sparkle and her girls from the S.H.P.. Raeven stayed with them. They were doing all kind of bad things but it didn't bother Raeven because she too had done the same before she met them. They started shoplifting and robbing kids who were coming home from school. They took turns taking the kids stuff and didn't care how they felt. They even robbed the Jittney man every time they got on there, just to have money to eat and smoke weed. But Raeven couldn't understand why those girls was on streets doing what they were doing. They all had homes to go to and people that loved them. But she never asked because she enjoyed being around them. They all had boyfriends. Raeven wasn't ready for a boyfriend yet. However, she decided to give it a try. But she was afraid. She started to a guy named Leonard. He was a lot older than her. Raeven was feeling him. He was the second guy that she really liked and cared about. Well at least she thought she did until he started talking to another girl named Jada; who was much older. That didn't bother Raeven though because she had practically given him away when she stopped talking to him.

After a while, her and Raeven became friends. They all was hanging out until they got into a fight with a girl named Monica. Monica tried to set Raeven up. Her and her auntie was trying to fight Raeven. But Rochelle wasn't having that. Rochelle came across the tracks.

"Raeven, you and Jada fina fight one on one! Get y'all

ass in the road!" Rochelle yelled. Jada was bigger then Raeven. But that didn't stop Raeven from fighting. Raeven didn't win but the next day, Sparkle saw Jada and beat the hell out of her. Everyone knew Raeven was too small for Jada. But Sparkle was the perfect match. Raeven liked staying over at Sparkle's house. But James didn't like it. He called the police on Raeven because he didn't want her in the hood.

"Raeven, you have to leave." The officer said.

"Ok. But my clothes is at Sparkle's grandma's house. Can I go get them?" I asked.

"Yes." The officer said.

Raeven went around the apartments and took off through the bushes. She waited it out until they left. No one knew where Raeven was. Again, she had out smarted them. She set there until ten o'clock that night. She dashed up the street and found Sparkle and the crew. They was happy to see her because they thought sure she was gone back to foster care. She promised herself that was one place she was not going back to. And she didn't.

One day, they caught her and she had to do forty five days in juvenile. When she got out, she moved in with Jewel. Raeven was on chill for a while until Jewel told her she needed to get a job to help her pay the bills. So, she started back selling drugs. During this time, Rhiley and Rochelle was dancing at a club and tricking. But that life wasn't for Raeven to live because she knew nothing about it. But her mind did inquiry.

"Rochelle how do you stay laced in all the new Jordans?" Raeven asked.

"Bishop hooks me up." She shrugged.

"Who is that?" Raeven asked.

"Just a nigga I trick with that works at Footlocker. If you want a pair all you got to do is make it do what it do."

Raeven couldn't build herself up to do it. Until one day, she was walking by the mall and she passed Footlocker. He was in there. Raeven kept walking but curiosity got the best of her. "Fuck it!" She said. She walked in. Bishop was skeptical because Raeven was dressed like a boy. But that didn't stop anything. They got it over with and Raeven walked out with a pair of Jordan's and a bag of other shit as well. When Raeven got home, she felt so bad about it.

"I can't believe I did that stupid shit." She shook her head.

"Tricking is tricking. No matter how you do it. It would be the same way if you tricked another way. Those shoes was $160. Let's not mention the pants, shirts and socks. Get over it." Jewel said.

"Ok." Raeven sighed.

Raeven had a boyfriend named Darrel. But he never knew because he was never home. Darrel was much older then Raeven. He was a drug dealer and he worked for Dade County. He was great guy but he was just like all men. A hoe. Raeven didn't care because she was a dog herself.

Chapter 9

Jewel's boyfriend brought a guy with him over. He was white and he liked Raeven. She wasn't into him. But he had money. He was a test to see if she could get his money. And she did!

One day, he placed a ring under a pillow while Raeven was in the bathroom. When she came out, he went in the bathroom and she laid down. Raeven placed her bad under the pillow and when she felt the ring, she got scared. She was young and not ready for that. She quickly placed the ring back under the pillow when she heard the bathroom door open.

"Raeven, I must admit you are the first woman I've

ever been with. You took my virginity."

"Yea but you wanted it more than I did." She said.

"That's because I've never had it. Plus the men at work always pick at me. That's why I wanted you but I think I've fallen in love with you. And I want to marry you." He admitted.

"No. I can't. I'm not ready."

"Well I can't go home like this. In my religion, we aren't allowed to have sex without getting married. So please keep the ring and think about it at least."

Raeven took the ring home and asked Jewel to put it up. She didn't want Darrel finding it. As time went by, she gave him an answer. She couldn't marry him. She was too young. So, she gave him back the ring. "Go find your wife. Because it's not me." He was sad. But everyday she regretted it because maybe her life would've been better.

Shortly after, Darrel found out. But dude was long go to New York. Raeven should have ran off with him. But she chose to stay in Miami, living the life that she lived. Darrel was her man but he was also everyone else's man. He cheated like crazy. He made sure his side women didn't mumble a word to Raeven. But Raeven was far from dumb. She was still messing with the guy Bishop from Footlocker. Bishop was a freak. He turned Raeven out. He turned her into a freak. He taught her things she never knew before she met him.

"I wonder why Bishop not answering any of my calls." Rochelle smirked.

"I don't know. Let me call him on three way." Raeven dialed his number. Bishop explained that he couldn't mess around with her no more. And that he had fallen in love with Raeven.

Shortly after, Raeven discovered that she was pregnant from him. She was about to lose her mind because she was just a baby herself. She was only nineteen years old.

"You got to get an abortion." Bishop said. "I'll pay for it."

"Ok." Raeven was with it. She was too young to have a baby. That was the purpose of her turning dude down who wanted to marry her. She just wasn't ready. So,

The Pain in Dade

she went home and told Cora.

"Raeven, if you kill this baby, I will never talk to you again! That is a sin before God!" Cora yelled. Jewel agreed. But Raeven wasn't hearing them. So, she went down to the clinic anyways.

When she got there, she was scared. She asked Darrel to wait outside because she didn't want him in there. As she walked to the back, she was coming up with a plan. Cora's words replayed in her mind. "A baby is a blessing from God." So, she knew she had to think quick.

"Do you like your job?" Raeven asked the doctor.

"I can't answer that. Because I'll lose my job." She answered. The doctor looked at Raeven then back at the papers in her hand. "Close door and have a seat." She said. "Listen, this job pays my bills. When I finish school, I plan on changing jobs because it goes against my religion." She admitted.

"Can you give me a fake receipt?" Raeven asked. The doctor knew exactly where she was going with this.

"I'm sorry. I can't. I don't want to lose my job."

Raeven respected her because she knew this was how she fed her family.

"Sit back there in the room and make sure this is what you really want while I take another patient." The doctor said.

Raeven sat in the back, thinking of what to do. The. She looked down at the receipt. It was empty. That had to be God. Raeven wrote a price on it. There was no way she was getting rid of her first born child. She got up and walked out like she was in pain as if she went through the process. But only if Darrel knew. He took her to Cora's house.

"Rochelle, let's go to the Flea Market so I can put some music in your car." Raeven said the minute Darrel left.

"Nope." She had attitude. Only because she thought Raeven had the abortion. They all did until she showed them the fake receipt. They still wasn't buying it. So Raeven had to go get a pregnancy test. When she took it, they all was happy. They went to the Flea Market. Raeven shopped for the baby and put music in Rochelle's car.

The Pain in Dade

As the months past, Darrel had not called. That showed Raeven just the kind of man he was. He was never in love. He just wanted to kill the baby. But Hod had other plans. September 30th, 1999, she gave birthday to a beautiful baby girl. She named her Feilisa. She brought so much joy to Raeven's heart and she was the happiest woman on Earth.

After a month, Darrel called. He wanted to speak with Raeven. Rochelle answered. "Why are you calling my little sister? She don't want to talk to you and I'm not going to tell her you called. You not about to hurt her again. All you care about is your damn self!"

"Hoe put Raeven on the phone!" He spat.

"She don't live here no more!" Rochelle spat.

"Where she live!" He yelled.

"That ain't no of your damn business! And another thing, she had the baby!"

"Yeah right! I got a receipt liar. She had an abortion!"

"Yeah believe that if you want dumb ass. That receipt fake. And if you want to see your baby, you come to my grandma house and I will take you to see your baby." Darrel had pissed her off. She forgot he didn't suppose to know about the baby until child support served him with those papers. But she was ticked off.

A week or so later, Rochelle called and asked Raeven if she could bring Darrel by to see the baby. "Wait, how does he know about the baby?" Raeven asked.

"He called and he was talking junk and it just slipped." She explained.

"Ok. Whatever. Yeah you can bring him."

When Raeven hung up the phone she was nervous. The last time she saw Darrel was the day he thought she had the abortion. Raeven still had feelings for him. She was young, dumb and full of cum. That was a way of saying she was stupid over him and he didn't give three fucks about her.

When they pulled up in his new truck, Raeven brought the baby out. Darrel looked at her. "This is a beautiful baby." He smiled. "But this not my baby. This a Arab baby."

"The DNA test will tell your fat ass the truth!" Raeven

spat.

Darrel left. He changed his name and it made it was hard for child support to find him. But that didn't bother Raeven because she had moved on with her life. She met a guy name Mark from Detroit. She was in love with him. Mark assured her that from this day forward, Feilisa was his daughter. "Fuck Darrel. Any man in their right mind would want to be her father. Look how beautiful she looks."

With him, Raeven had no worries. He was a hustler. He sold drugs and she was working the stores. Mark would come home early and make sure Feilisa took a bath, ate and was in bed; ready for daycare the next morning. Meanwhile, Raeven was out working the stores with her partners. One of them will have the merchandise on them and walk out. While the other would target attention from the sales clerk to make it seem as if they are the ones with the stolen merchandise. Basically giving the salesclerk a run for their money by throwing them completely off. That was their scam for a while. Then, they started stealing the merchandise, then returning it with the tag attached to get the money. Raeven and the crew was making grands. They was doing better than the drop boys. Then one day they was going out of town and this undercover started following them. Raeven was scared. She caught the Greyhound back home. What they was doing, was Fed time. And she didn't want to be separated from her child. So, she quit and found a real job. She saw herself getting locked up and not getting out. The money she had saved up to take care her daughter, she gave to Mark to flip so they wouldn't run out. They was a team. She knew it wasn't any better but they had to eat and keep a roof over their head.

Then one day, Rhiley asked her to come to the club. Raeven was a tomboy. She knew nothing about dancing in heels but she could dance her ass off. So, she reluctantly went. When they arrived to the club, there was this tall woman by the name of Goldyn who was helping Rhiley. There was also a bartender named Mita who gave Raeven a shot of 151. There was three guys sitting in front of the stage. Two were black and one was white.

The Pain in Dade

"That's the one you focus on." Mita pointed at the white man. "That's the one that will spend. Them black muthafuckas don't like to come up off that dollar." Raeven took note to everything Mita said.

On Raeven's first night, she made one hundred and fifty dollars. They all told her that was good because some girls don't even make that. "Why women on the street say they be making thousands of dollars?" Raeven asked.

"Because they be sucking and fucking in the club." Rhiley smirked.

"I knew they was doing something extra." Raeven said. And that's one thing she wasn't doing. Hell, she didn't want to dance but she needed the money.

Chapter 10

As time went on, Raeven started talking to Nick. She was in love with him until she got pregnant and moved to Atlanta. On the Fourth of July, Rhiley called Raeven and told her Rochelle was fucking Nick. Raeven didn't want to believe it. So she came home to see it for herself. It was true. Nick tried to convince Raeven that it had just happened but Raeven knew better.

"That's why your baby going to be my step daughter and niece!" Rochelle yelled. Raeven wanted to kill her. But she let them have each other. She moved away and had her baby. When Liyah was born, Raeven let a guy named Jasper take a DNA test. He told Raeven, the results said it was his child. But when she saw the papers, the papers looked fake. So, she asked this police from around the hood to take a look at the papers. He assured her the papers were indeed fake and that she needed to take him to court. But Raeven didn't have money to file a motion. She wasn't working in the club no more because she couldn't be around Rochelle. So, she went back to the stores with Sparkle and the click.

Raeven lived with her cousins Lil Pooh, Tess and her boyfriend Robert. They was getting along on and off. They was one big family. When her and Robert broke up, she started talking to this dope boy named King. He was fine. He had a black Lexus. They were preparing to go out to eat and to the movies. Raeven was in the house getting dressed. Lil Pooh had called Robert and told him about the date.

"Hurry up King. We need to leave before Robert get here." King was a little scared.

"Meet me down the street." King said.

Raeven was mad because she had to walk down the street. She was praying she didn't see Robert. She spotted King driving by. "Where the hell he going?" She asked herself. When Raeven got to the road, she saw Robert. "Fuck!" She spat.

"Oh, so you got a date huh? Lil Pooh called and told me you going on a date. You out here in your lil Levi skirt and shit!" He yelled as he walked up on her.

Raeven wanted to beat Lil Pooh ass. All the shit she had done for Pooh and she go back and snitch. "Yeah I'm going on a date. Nigga did you forget that you broke up with me? Why you worried about it!" Raeven spat.

"I bet that Nigga ain't going to stop and pick you up!" Robert barked. And King didn't. He kept going. Robert reached under her skirt and felt that she didn't have on any panties. He got even madder. "Oh so he was going to fuck too!" Truth of the matter, Raeven didn't plan on having sex with King. She just was rushing to get dressed and forgot to put panties on. "Get your ass in the house!" Raeven didn't want to go in but she didn't want to fight with him either. So she went inside. Robert apologized and they made love to make up. Then they fell asleep.

The Pain in Dade

The next day, when Raeven saw Pooh she asked her why she snitched on her. Raeven wouldn't have ever did her like that. She tried her best to make Raeven believe she didn't tell Robert. But Raeven knew she did. So, she let it go. She knew Pooh would need her one day. They was blood cousins and they was supposed to stick together.

But back to work with Sparkle. Raeven knew they had money to get. It wasn't right but she had to keep a roof over her kids head. She made more money stealing than working at McDonalds or anywhere else. They hit every store on US1. No one couldn't understand how they were getting the clothes out the store. They were professionals when it came to stealing. They knew exactly who was the store cops and they dodged their ass. On several occasions, they would take the clothes back to the store with the receipts. It was six of them in the crew. They racked up at least a grand a piece. On one occasion, the store ran out of money and they had to go to the back in the safe to get money. The manager was so angry because he couldn't understand how this even happened. The store had to close earlier than usual. Raeven them was back and forth out of town. From Jacksonville to Georgia. They will hit up their stores and get a hotel in the area just to rest. On their way home, they would work the stores that was on the way. They stopped at Dolphin Mall. They was dressed as if they were coming to shop, in hopes of not looking suspicious. They walked in as if they didn't know each other, grabbing the complementary shopping bags. When they filled their bags up, they sent each other a text. As well as their driver who was waiting at the door. They ran out of the store with lot of dresses that cost damn near three hundred dollars. Raeven had two bags full of them and so did the others who ran out with her. They had took the tag off their get away car so the police couldn't have a tag number to trace back. Once out of the area, they go to BCC and take all of the alarms off the dresses. After that was done, they sent different people back to the stores with the merchandise to get the money back. Raeven and her crew had a way of outsmarting the clerks. But when it starting becoming a piece of cake, she became scared. The very last time was when they went out of town and a black DT car was following them. They knew they time had come to an end. They was all in the car praying to God they didn't get caught. They didn't want the DT to catch them with the stolen merchandise on them. So they went to a hotel and got a room so that he could get off their trail.

Then the bad luck hit them. Sparkle and her boyfriend get into a fight. He gets arrested, they tow the car, leaving Raeven and the rest stranded in a town that they know nothing about. But their survivor mode instantly kicked in. They racked up some more money to get another car. They came up with enough money to even bond Sparkle's boyfriend out of jail. Sparkle was happy he was out, but they needed more money. She called her sister up to send them money to get back home.

"Look Sparkle, enough is enough. I quit. I'm not going back down this road again. I can't go to jail. I have to be out to raise my kids." Raeven said.

Sparkle was ok with Raeven's decision. She put together another crew. But not long after, they got caught for not listening. Usually when Raeven them walked in the stores, they kept their head down so the camera couldn't see their face. But this new click showed their faces to the camera. Sparkle sat down for a while until things cooled off. She had to pay out lots of money to bond them out.

Nonetheless, Raeven started back working at the club for a short period of time. She grew tired of that lifestyle as well. Her daughter was getting older and she didn't want her to know what she was out here doing. So, she called up her cousin Myah in Georgia to find out how the living was up there. Raeven had grew tired of sleeping from pillow to post. She wanted her own place. She knew if she put her mind to it, she could do it.

Raeven's cousin Taylor was in Miami visiting one weekend. She knew her only chance at change was catching a ride back with Taylor. Taylor agreed to take her back with her. But instead of taking her to Myah's house, she took her to her house. Raeven didn't want to go to Taylor's house. She wanted to go to Myah's. But Raeven stayed with her until Taylor was evicted, then neither one of them had anywhere to go.

Thankfully, the lady Ms. Brenda she was renting

The Pain in Dade

furniture from said they could stay at her house. "Y'all don't ask this lady for no food." Taylor warned Raeven and her son. Raven them was hungry.

One morning the lady walked in and asked Raeven if she knew how to cook. "Yeah I can."

"We'll go cook us something to eat." She said.

"I can't. My cousin said we can't eat your food." Raeven admitted.

"Baby, I'm a giving person. And y'all need to eat." She said with a warm smile. So, Raeven went in the kitchen and started cooking. Tyler was scared because he knew Taylor was going to be mad as hell. But Raeven didn't give a damn. She was pregnant and she had to eat.

The door opened and Taylor walked in. "Didn't I tell y'all not to eat this woman food!" She yelled.

"We didn't. She came and told us to come cook us something. Plus I'm pregnant. I can't sit around and starve." Raeven yelled back.

Taylor instantly got upset and they started fighting. Because she was the big cousin, Taylor wanted Raeven to be scared of her. But she wasn't. They wasn't kids. And they both was pregnant. "Y'all cut this foolishness out! I told that child to come in here and cook Taylor. It's not that big of a deal." Ms. Brenda said as she broke them apart. Taylor was angry. She packed up her and her kids and left. Raeven didn't have a clue of where she was going. Raeven sat down for a minute to talk to Ms. Brenda. After she managed to calm down, she got up and fixed them both a plate. After she finished eating, she washed the dishes and laid down. Raeven couldn't sleep because she didn't know where Taylor was. She was worried.

"May I use your phone?"

"Of course baby." Brenda handed her the phone. Raeven called James to let him know what happened. He informed her that Taylor had made it to Miami.

"What! And left me here! What am I supposed to do Daddy!" Raeven yelled. Ms. Brenda took the phone. James gave her Myah's number. Myah didn't live too far from Brenda.

"If you move up here, you can live with me Raeven. It won't be a problem." Brenda said. Raeven was uneasy because she didn't know Brenda too well. She wanted to be with her family. So Myah asked Brenda to meet her at the Piggly Wiggly. Raeven packed up her things and they left.

"Thanks for all that you have done for me. I really appreciate it." Raeven hugged Ms. Brenda.

"You're welcome. I was trying to get her to stay with me. But I understand that she wanted to be with her family." The lady looked over at Myah and smiled. They offered Ms. Brenda gas money but she refused it.

After a few weeks, Raeven moved in with Lil Pooh. Myah had too many people living with her. And even though Pooh had snitched on her, they still were the best of cousins. Pooh lived in the projects and that's a lifestyle Raeven wanted to run from. So, Raeven lived with her until she got on her feet.

Chapter 11

Stacey, one of Raeven's cousins had moved to Atlanta and Raeven moved with her. She got a job at CVS. She was doing really good and making money. One day on her off day, she was home chilling and Stacey's husband Jermaine and Lil Tom was there with her. Jermaine began getting fresh with Raeven. He even offered her money to have sex with him.

"Leave me the hell alone!" Raeven spat. But Jermaine didn't pay her any mind. He continued his charade.

"I'm telling Stacey!"

"Like she going to believe you!" He yelled.

The Pain in Dade

"Oh somebody will." Raeven snuck and called Jewel.

"He did what!" Jewel was angry. "Come here. Find a way here now."

When Stacey got home, Raeven told her to take her to the bus station. Raeven knew she couldn't stay there any longer. "Why?" Stacey asked. Raeven didn't know what to say.

"I just want to live with Jewel. She think that it's best. I don't think I'm going to make it up here." She lied.

"I feel you. Well if it don't work out in Mississippi, you can always come back."

Raeven wasn't coming back. She caught the bus to Brookhaven Mississippi. Jewel came and picked her up from the station and they drove to Monticello Mississippi. Jewel lived in the projects too. But it wasn't like Miami projects. So, Raeven just stuck it out. She loved with Jewel for three weeks. The manager had given Raeven her own place. She knew it had to be God. She was tired of staying with people. God had blessed her.

One day, Raeven's baby girl had ran out of her

medication. She had to go to the hospital. Surprisingly, they took her six month old daughter Liyah and placed her in foster care. She didn't understand why. They didn't take Feilisa. Raeven knew it was the black woman behind this.

Eventually, they gave her back. Later Raeven's sister discovered they was taking the babies, selling them to these white women who could not have babies. They placed Liyah in the hands of a woman who was Raeven's sister aunt. Luckily, she brought Liyah right to Raeven.

"Leave this state! They are trying to sell your baby to a woman who can't have kids." She said.

Raeven left. She packed her babies up and headed back to Miami. She put the girls in Cora's custody so they couldn't be taken. Raeven moved around for a while and then moved back to Georgia. She stayed in Augusta for nine years. Then moved back to Statesboro. There, she met a guy name Brock. He was much older. He was a good man. But not for her. He was too soft. He allowed her to walk all over him. He gave her anything she wanted. That was not the kind

The Pain in Dade

of man she was looking for. She had told everyone the moment she found her Prince Charming, she was going to marry him. But Brock was not it.

One day out of the blue, the kids father got in contact with her. "Hey Raeven. How are you?" He asked.

"I'm fine. What's up?" She said.

"Nothing much. You crossed my mind. I'm staying in Memphis. I want you and the kids to come move with me. I want us to get married. I want us to raise the kids together." He explained.

Raeven fell for the words that sounded sweet to her ears. She believed him. Thinking he had changed. Raeven lied and told her then boyfriend she was moving back to Miami but she was going to Mississippi.

He told Raeven he lived in Memphis until she was in route there. Then he told her he lived in Atlanta. So, she was on her way. They had two kids together and she knew this was the right thing to do. But he still wasn't her Prince Charming. She was forcing herself to love him all over again. But it didn't work. They both had skeletons in their closet. She knew she was going to hurt him bad because of the fact that he had fucked Rochelle and was bragging about it. When she told him how she felt, he didn't care about her feelings.

"Look, your brother inbox me saying he liked me since I moved here in the house. I told him I was with you. He said I was with the wrong brother and I wouldn't have nothing to worry about." Raeven showed him the messages.

Before Raeven tricked with him, she called her best friend to get advice. "Girl that nigga don't give a fuck about you! Do it! Did he care when he did it to you! You just paying him back!"

It took Raeven a while to give in because she knew it was wrong. But she needed that money and she did it. She was only going to do it once. But once turned into three times. His head game was fire. The best she had ever had.

When Nick called, Raeven and his brother was in the hotel room. While his brother gave her head, she was on the phone with Nick. Raeven felt like a pimp all over again. When she told him where she was, he jumped up and started crying. Raeven knew she was wrong but Nick had drug her through the mill when she was young. He hurt her. Nick never thought Raeven would do anything like that. She was always different from her sisters. They had a I don't give a fuck attitude. They would sleep with your mom, daddy, your brother and sister. They just didn't a damn. When Nick slept with Rochelle, Raeven was hurt. She couldn't take it. So when his brother came to her, he couldn't take it. His brother told Raeven a woman was suppose to be treated with respect. She was touched by that.

Raeven didn't just sleep with Nick's brother. She was in a need of money. He was paying big cash and she went for it. She had kids to take care of. She was a go getter. His dick was small but his head was great! He needed something to make up for his small dick. But the money was better.

When Raeven left Miami to go back up, it hit her. "Did he feel like that when he slept with Rochelle?" She thought to herself. He didn't care one bit. When they got on the elevator, Nick called. So he wouldn't hear the elevator bell, Raeven waited to answer and got off.

"Where are you?" Nick asked.

"At my grandma's house." She lied. "Listen, I need rest. I can't talk tonight. I will call you in the morning." He knew something was up because they would usually talk on the phone until they fall asleep.

Raeven went back in the room with his brother and fell asleep. The next morning, he gave her $350. "I wish you stay here in Miami. I'm in love with you Raeven." Raeven knew he had lost his mind. This was just business. All she knew was to trick and get money. Not fall for the lovey dicey shit.

He took her to Cora's house. Rochelle went and got the rental car to go to Statesboro Georgia. Raeven had to get her girls and her clothes. Her ex boyfriend begged her to stay with him but she had to go. She couldn't be with him.

On her way to Mississippi, even Sparkle told her not to go. They knew he didn't change. They was right.

The Pain in Dade

He was still bossy. Raeven didn't stay with him long. She was ready to go back to Georgia….

The Final Chapter

Raeven found her a country man and fell in love with him. That's who she is with today. He changed her a lot. She changed herself. She had to become a role model for her kids. She decided to stay in Mississippi. The goal was to get her life right and she did.

Raeven stopped moving the kids around. God has blessed her with a job working at Valley Tool ; with the best team of people ever. She learned how to have friends and family. Some may think she's a bit crazy but she's the most loving person ever. God has changed her for the better. And she thank him daily for that.